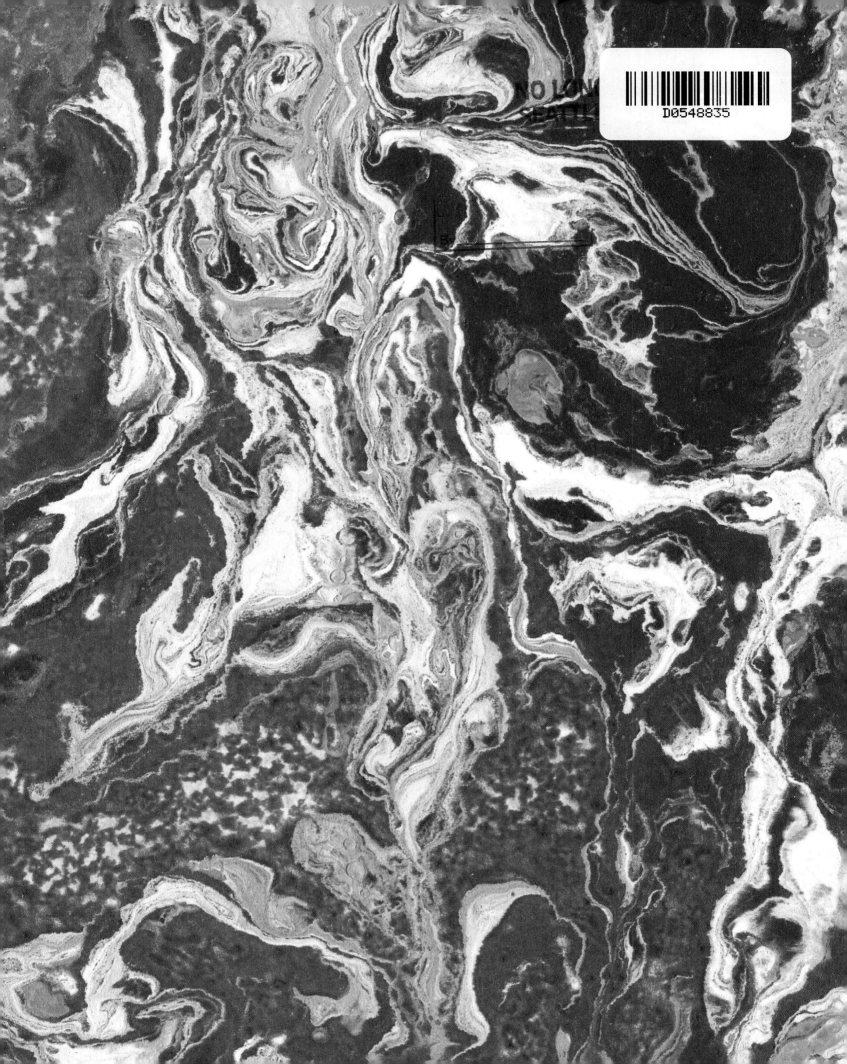

TO THE ANGEL ISLAND CONSERVANCY FOR ITS DEDICATION TO PRESERVING,
RESTORING, AND BUILDING COMMUNITY SUPPORT FOR ANGEL ISLAND,
AND TO THE ANGEL ISLAND STATE PARK STAFF.—C.A.

THANK YOU TO CASEY DEXTER-LEE, THE ANGEL ISLAND STATE PARK INTERPRETER;
LAURA WOOD, AN ARCHITECT FOR THE CALIFORNIA STATE PARKS;
AND NOAH M. STEWART, HISTORIAN FOR THE CALIFORNIA STATE PARKS.
I'D ALSO LIKE TO THANK MY FAMILY: JACOB, MICA, AND CALDER.—R.S.

Text copyright © 2022 Caroline Arnold
Illustration copyright © 2022 Rachell Sumpter

Illustration of Juliet Fish Nichols courtesy of the *San Francisco Call*, Sunday, June 15, 1890
Illustration of "Juliet Fish Nichols: The Real Heroine of Angel Island" courtesy of the *San Francisco Chronicle*, Sunday, May 13, 1906
Map of Angel Island from *Angel Island: The Ellis Island of the West* by Mary Bamford, published by the Woman's American Baptist Home Mission Society in May 1917
Photo of Angel Island Lighthouse courtesy of the U.S. Coast Guard
Case and endpaper images courtesy of Shutterstock

Book design by Melissa Nelson Greenberg

Published in 2022 by CAMERON + COMPANY, a division of ABRAMS.

Library of Congress Cataloging-in-Publication Data available.
ISBN: 978-1-951836-37-5

Printed in China .

10 9 8 7 6 5 4 3 2 1

CAMERON KIDS is an imprint of CAMERON + COMPANY

CAMERON + COMPANY
Petaluma, California
www.cameronbooks.com

KEEPER OF THE LIGHT

JULIET FISH NICHOLS FIGHTS THE SAN FRANCISCO FOG

Written by CAROLINE ARNOLD

Illustrated by RACHELL SUMPTER

cameron kids

JOURNAL OF Light Station, Angel Island, San Francisco Bay, California

Juliet F. Nichols, Keeper

RECORD OF IMPORTANT EVENTS AT THE STATION, BAD WEATHER, ETC.

September 1, 1902. Clear skies, light wind, very warm.

I, Juliet Fish Nichols, am the new keeper of the Angel Island Light.

Day and night — summer, fall, winter, spring — I must keep the light shining and the fog bell ringing, no matter what.

Today the fog, my foe, is far away. The city sparkles in the sunlight. Boats dance on the bay. I wave to a ferry on its way over to San Francisco. It toots its horn in reply.

At sunset, I light the lamp and hang it in front of the bell house. Bright beams flash on the water. I set my clock to check the lamp at midnight.

Another light blinks on nearby Alcatraz Island, home to a squadron of pelicans. While they sleep, the two lights will guide ships safely to the harbor.

September 2, 1902. Overcast, light wind, very hazy.

Mornings, I take down the lamp, fill it with oil, and polish the glass until it gleams. I tidy my small house and write in my log. Outside, sea lions bark and gulls squawk overhead.

Duties done, I climb the 151 steps to the top of the cliff and take the path past the fort. The soldiers are my only neighbors, except for the blacksmith and his wife over the hill.

At the top of the hill, wind tugs at my long skirt. Far away a fogbank lurks. When the fog and I meet, I will be ready.

Today, fog pushes through the Golden Gate, spilling over the headlands and into the bay. It swallows sailing ships, freighters, ferries, and steamboats. It's time.

I grab the crank of the fog bell machine and turn it to tighten the chain. As it unwinds, a mallet strikes the giant bell.

CLANG! CLANG! Two loud rings every fifteen seconds warn passing ships to keep away from the rocks.

Four hours later, the fog is still thick. I wind the chain again and again until the fog lifts, floats away. I get little sleep.

November 4, 1902. Southeast storm with rain and hail.

Days grow short. Winter rains begin.

I write to Mother, stationed just down the coast above the wide Pacific. We are both lighthouse keepers! When the rain lets up, I put on a slicker and walk to the post office.

December 13, 1902. Rain, calm. Later, drifting fog.

Cold, thick fog wraps around my house. The bell rings.

January 16, 1903. Southern gale with heavy rain.

Raindrops clatter off my roof into the rain barrel. After hanging the lamp, I put an extra lump of coal in the stove and curl up with a book. While the storm rages, I read about ostriches, cheetahs, and hyenas in Africa…

February 28, 1903. Fresh north wind, clear, very cold.
I catch the boat to the city to shop for supplies, returning in time to hang the light for the night. In my basket: apples, flour, sugar, beans, and seeds for my garden.

March 21, 1903. Clear, calm, sunny, warm.

Spring flowers cover the hillside. Golden poppies turn their faces to the sun.
I dig a small patch of dirt and plant lettuce, cabbage, beets, and peas.

Day after day, month after month, I watch the weather and keep the
light shining, the bell ringing. The fog and I keep each other company.
Three years pass quickly by.

Until...

April 18, 1906. Calm, hazy. Just before dawn.

I awake with a jolt. Everything is moving!

My bed thrashes like a boat in a storm. Dishes smash. Outside,
the lamp swings wildly on its hook. I hang on for dear life and wish
I were not so alone.

When the shaking stops, I inspect the house —

Storehouse cracked. Stone basement badly cracked. House plaster cracked.

— Luckily, nothing that can't be fixed.

But when I aim my telescope at San Francisco, my heart sinks. Tall buildings have fallen down to the ground. Flames leap up into the sky. Smoke billows over my broken city.

The soldiers at the fort leave to fight the fires and help restore order.

For three long days the fires rage. Ferries crisscross the bay, taking people to safety. At night, I hang my lamp to guide their way.

June 3, 1906. Distant threatening fog.

Workmen come to repair the lighthouse. While they hammer, swallows chirp in their nest under the eaves. I pick lettuce from my garden to make salad for supper.

June 22, 1906. Fresh southwest wind, hazy.

Ships crowd the bay as they make their way to the harbor, their decks piled high with building supplies.

As darkness falls, scattered lights flicker on in the city. Fog lingers outside the Golden Gate.

July 2, 1906. Fog, light southwest wind.

At midday, fog creeps low over the water. Like ghosts,
the boats slowly disappear from view.

I wind up the bell machine.

CLANG! CLANG!

Fifteen seconds later the mallet strikes again.

CLANG! CLANG!

Then, suddenly . . . silence.

Something is wrong!

I turn the crank again, but the bell does not ring!

I dash off a telegram to the lighthouse engineer's office in San Francisco.

TAP! TAP! Machinery disabled. **TAP! TAP!**

Need repairs now!

Fog is growing thicker by the minute.

And the boat with the repairman will not come until morning.

There is no time to climb the 151 steps and run for help.

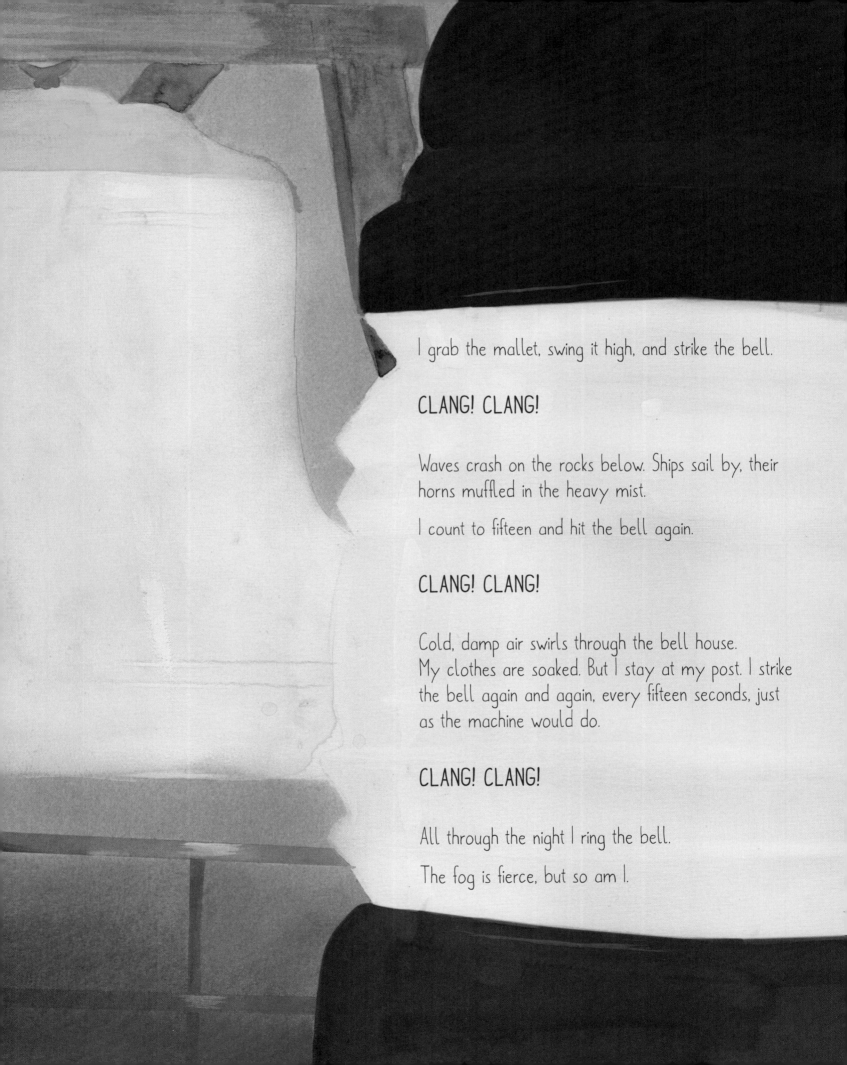

I grab the mallet, swing it high, and strike the bell.

CLANG! CLANG!

Waves crash on the rocks below. Ships sail by, their horns muffled in the heavy mist.

I count to fifteen and hit the bell again.

CLANG! CLANG!

Cold, damp air swirls through the bell house. My clothes are soaked. But I stay at my post. I strike the bell again and again, every fifteen seconds, just as the machine would do.

CLANG! CLANG!

All through the night I ring the bell.

The fog is fierce, but so am I.

July 3, 1906. Dense fog, then clearing.

After twenty hours and thirty-five minutes, the fog begins to lift. Headlands peek through the morning light. Boats reappear on the water.

I ring the bell one last time—

CLANG! CLANG!

And then I let the mallet drop. My body aches from head to toe. My dress is drenched. But I made it through the night. The fog is gone.

The ships are safe. But for how long?

July 4, 1906. Calm, clear. Distant fog.

I raise the flag for Independence Day. There will be no fireworks.

Today the fog, my foe, is far away. But I'm still here.

I, Juliet Fish Nichols, am keeper of the Angel Island Light. Day and night — summer, fall, winter, spring — I keep the light shining and the fog bell ringing, no matter what.

JULIET FISH NICHOLS

Keeper of the Light is a fictionalized account based on true events and historical documents about Juliet Fish Nichols, keeper of the Angel Island Light Station in San Francisco Bay from 1902–1914.

Juliet Fish Nichols (1859–1947) grew up in Oakland, California. In 1888, she married Commander Henry Nichols of the US Navy. He later became superintendent of the 12th Light-House District along the coast of California. In 1891, after Juliet's father died, Henry helped Juliet's mother, Emily Fish, obtain a job as lighthouse keeper at Point Pinos in Pacific Grove, California. In addition to performing her duties as keeper, Emily often entertained guests at the lighthouse. Henry Nichols died in 1899, leaving Juliet without permanent financial support. When Juliet learned that the lighthouse keeper at Point Knox on Angel Island was retiring, she applied for the job. She was forty-three years old. In contrast to her mother, Juliet lived a quiet life at her lighthouse, rarely receiving visitors. After retiring, she lived the rest of her life in Oakland, not far from San Francisco Bay and Angel Island.

On the evening of July 4, 1906, just two days after Juliet's heroic ringing of the fog bell by hand, the machine broke again! Once more Juliet struck the bell herself, this time for eight long hours, using a hammer from the toolbox. The Lighthouse Board in Washington, D.C., sent her a letter commending her for her outstanding dedication to duty on the foggy days and nights between July 2 and July 5, 1906. Without Juliet's bell to guide them, the boat traffic in San Francisco Bay could easily have met disaster. In 1960, after a new light station was built at Point Blunt on Angel Island, the Point Knox lighthouse station was closed, and the house where Juliet once lived burned down. The giant bell, too heavy to move, remains at Point Knox. It is a reminder of Juliet Fish Nichols's heroic efforts to keep the bell ringing in the foggy summer days after the terrible San Francisco earthquake of 1906.

THE REAL HEROINE OF ANGEL ISLAND

HOW PLUCKY MRS NICHOLS WOUND UP THE FOG BELL MACHINERY EVERY FIFTY MINUTES FOR SEVENTY TWO HOURS AND SAVED SHIPS IN GOLDEN GATE FROM RUNNING ON THE ROCKS

The logs of the Light and Fog Bell Station on Angel Island, San Francisco Bay, in which Juliet recorded the events of each day, are housed at the National Archives in Washington, D.C. Excerpts from Juliet's log can be found on the author's website, www.carolinearnoldbooks.com/angelisland.html. A bibliography, list of further reading, and more information about Juliet Fish Nichols and the Point Knox light station are also on the website.

ANGEL ISLAND

At 1.2 square miles, Angel Island is the largest island in San Francisco Bay. When Juan Manuel de Ayala y Aranza, the first European to visit the island, arrived in 1775, he encountered the indigenous Miwoks, who had been coming there to hunt, fish, and gather acorns and other wild plants for thousands of years. Over the next half century, the regional Miwok population was decimated due to resettlement and introduced diseases, and their use of the island as a hunting ground ended. In 1848 at the end of the Mexican–American War, California became part of the United States. Two years later, the federal government became the official owner of Angel Island.

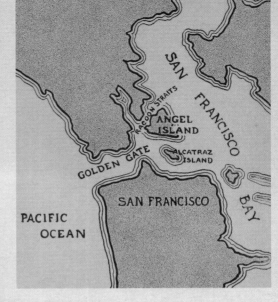

During Juliet's years as lighthouse keeper, Angel Island was used as an Army base (Fort McDowell), a quarantine station, and an immigration station. The quarantine station at Ayala Cove was put into operation in 1891. Overseas passengers arriving in San Francisco who were suspected of having infectious diseases, such as smallpox, were brought there before being allowed to enter the United States. They were examined, quarantined in barracks, and treated if necessary, and their belongings were disinfected. The immigration station, opened in 1910, was on the east side of the island. As the West Coast's primary immigration facility, immigrants, mainly from China and Japan, were brought there to be examined and interrogated, often being detained for weeks, months, or even years, and in many cases deported. At the time, US government policy discriminated against Asian immigration. The station closed in 1940, when operations moved to the mainland. The Army left Angel Island in 1946 but returned in 1954 to install a Nike missile site. It was removed in 1962, and military use of the island ended. At the urging of a citizens' group, Angel Island became a state park open to the public.

To learn more about Angel Island, go to: Angel Island Conservancy, http://angelisland.org; Angel Island State Park, https://www.parks.ca.gov/?page_id=468

LIGHTHOUSE AT POINT KNOX

The light station at Point Knox, on a rocky outcropping on the southwest corner of Angel Island, was the first of the island's three lighthouses. It consisted of a small house for the keeper, storage buildings, and a bell house. Starting in 1886 as a fog bell station, its three-thousand-pound bronze bell was mounted on a platform above the water. A heavy weight suspended below the platform powered a mallet that struck the bell. In 1900, a light was added to the station. When lit, it could be seen up to thirteen miles away. On clear nights, the lighted lamp hung at the front of the bell house; during the day, it was brought back into the bell house with a pulley. On foggy days and nights, the light was useless. Then the sound of the bell warned ships to keep away from the shore.

To learn more about the Point Knox lighthouse, go to: https://www.lighthousefriends.com/light.asp?ID=337

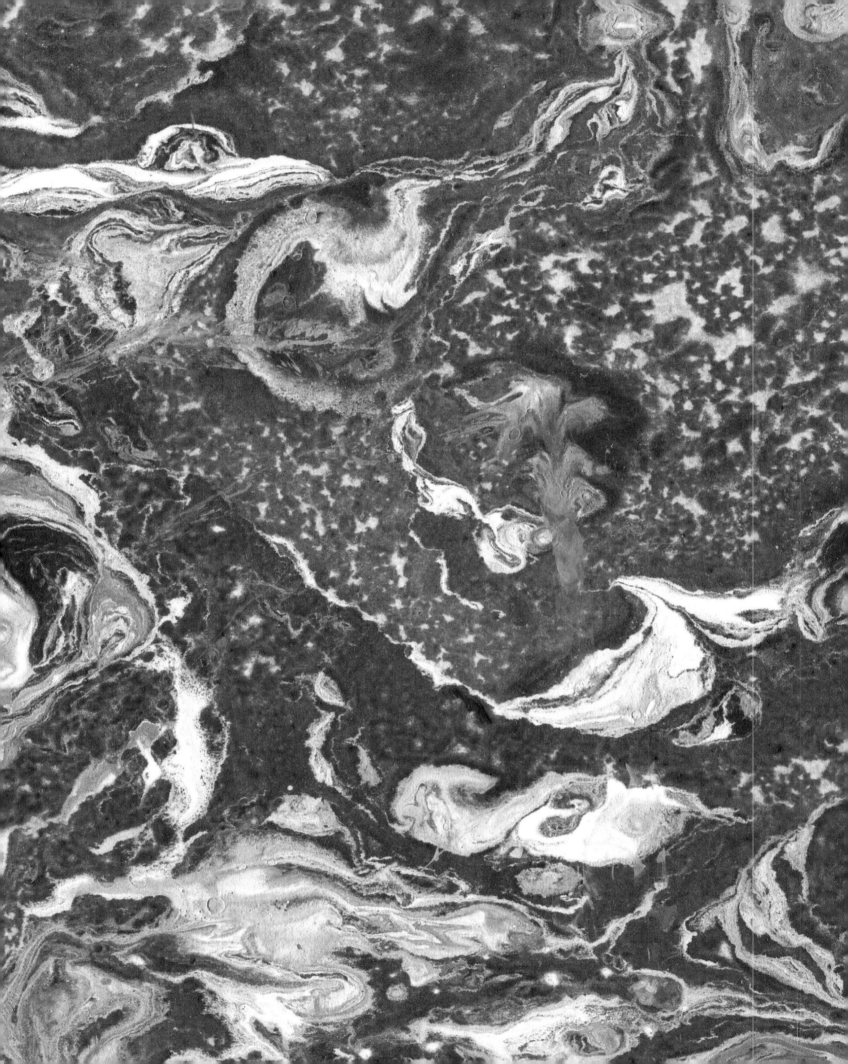